Printed in the United States of America.

Library of Congress Catalog Card Number: 95-68629
ISBN 0-7868-1443-8

Book design by Matthew Van Fleet.

CONSIDER the FOLLOWING

A way cool set of science questions, answers, and ideas to ponder